Stephen Gammell

Once Upon MacDonald's Farm...

Four Winds Press
Macmillan Publishing Company
New York
Collier Macmillan Publishers
London

Macmillan Publishing Company
866 Third Avenue, New York, N.Y. 10022
Collier Macmillan Canada, Inc.
Printed in the United States of America
11 10 9 8 7 6 5 4 3

LIBRARY OF CONGRESS CATALOGING IN PUBLICATION DATA
GAMMELL, STEPHEN.
Once upon MacDonald's farm.
Summary: MacDonald tries farming with exotic circus
animals, but has better luck with his neighbor's cow,
horse, and chicken.
1. Children's stories, American. [1. Farm life --
Fiction. 2. Animals--Fiction] I. Title.
[PZ7. G1440n 1985] [E] 84-29356
ISBN 0-02-737210-3

To my dear One,
my family
and Sully...

While it is true that MacDonald had a farm...

it wasn't much of a farm,

and he had no animals.
None at all.

"I really must have some animals..."

So, he bought an elephant....

he also bought a baboon
and a lion.

In the morning, MacDonald and the elephant went out to the field...

to do the plowing.

Much later that afternoon,

there were still some chores
to be done.

Eggs to gather...

Milking to do...

MacDonald was weary, and
went to bed early.

But while he slept, the animals decided to leave. And did...

without a sound.

When MacDonald awoke, he had no animals...

but his neighbor offered
to help.

That evening, he sent over
a horse, a cow and a chicken.

MacDonald was thankful for his new animals.

So, after a good sleep and a healthy breakfast, he was eager to start work.

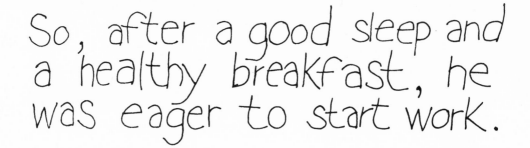

He had eggs to gather, the milking to do...

But first the plowing.